Travel

By Sally Cowan

T0342779

Contents

Travel: At Home or Overseas

Most families like to travel together and share exciting experiences. But is it better for children to see their own country or to travel overseas?

Lots of children do not like travelling overseas on long plane trips. They find it more fun to travel short distances by car or bike in their own country.

This type of travel does not cost as much as holidays overseas, either. It also allows families to take more holidays, or have friends join them.

Many children like to go to the beach or the countryside for their holidays. Others like to visit amusement parks and zoos, and go to the movies. There is no need to travel overseas to go to these places.

Parents often think their children would enjoy overseas travel, and learn more from it, when the children are older.

However, there are many children who enjoy travelling to other countries. During the long plane flight, they watch movies or play video games and the journey passes quickly.

Children who like to travel overseas say that there are so many new sights and sounds to experience in a different country.

It is exciting to visit huge castles. The children enjoy imagining what it would have been like to have lived there long ago.

They also enjoy trying to speak a different language.

Some children develop new interests in the music and dance of the countries that they visit. When they return home, many children take up new hobbies.

Spanish flamenco dancers

It is important for children to have great experiences and to have fun when they travel with their family and friends. They can do this whether they travel in their own country or overseas.

Make a Travel Brochure

Goal

To use a computer to make a two-page travel brochure. The brochure should attract tourists to a favourite place not far from where you live.

Materials

- computer

- photos of places to stay

- digital camera

- paper

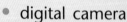

- photos of the place

- printer

- map of the place

Steps

1. Decide which place to write about. Carefully plan the information that will go in the brochure. Think about what tourists can see and do there. Make notes about special places to visit and activities to do.

2. Use the camera to take photos of the places and activities.

3. Decide on a title for the brochure. It could be the name of the place. Include a brief slogan. Choose special fonts and bright colours to attract readers.

4. Select the best photo and insert it under the title and slogan.

5. List the reasons why people might like to visit the place. Use short sentences and a clear font that can be read easily. Add some smaller photos to go with the sentences.

Visit Bluehaven
for a great beach holiday!

Play on the sandy beaches.

Swim or surf in the waves.

Visit the wildlife sanctuary.

Climb the lighthouse at Rocky Point.

6. Make a new page. Type the heading "How to get there".

7. Tell readers how they can travel to the place. Insert the map and mark the place on the map with an arrow and label.

8. Type the heading "Where to stay".

9. Insert photos of motels, houses or other places to stay. Type the phone number and website for tourists to get information.

How to get there

Bluehaven is a two-hour drive from the city of Claybourne.
Take the Grand Coastal Highway or catch a bus. Buses leave Central
Station every hour. Check the website at *www.bluehavenbus.com*
for timetables.

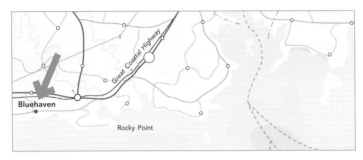

Where to stay

Houses and motels

Camping and caravan park

For more information phone Bluehaven Accommodation
on 9234 5678, or visit *www.bluehavenaccommodation.com*.

10. Print out the brochure in colour. If possible, use both sides of the paper.

Visit Bluehaven
for a great beach holiday!

Play on the sandy beaches.

Swim or surf in the waves.

Visit the wildlife sanctuary.

Climb the lighthouse at Rocky Point.